CUP GLORY

LEARNING RESOURCES

First published in 2013 by Wayland

Text copyright © Alan Durant 2013
Illustrations © Wayland 2013

Wayland
338 Euston Road
London NW1 3BH

Wayland Australia
Level 17/207 Kent Street
Sydney, NSW 2000

Series Editor: Victoria Brooker
Series design: Robert Walster and Basement68
Cover design: Lisa Peacock
Consultant: Dee Reid

A CIP catalogue record for this book is available
from the British Library.
Dewey number: 823.9'2-dc23

ISBN 978 0 7502 7985 7

2 4 6 8 10 9 7 5 3 1

Printed in China

Wayland is a division of Hachette Children's Books,
an Hachette UK Company
www.hachette.co.uk

FOOTBALL FACTOR

CUP GLORY

Alan Durant and Andrew Chiu

WAYLAND

www.waylandbooks.co.uk

It was Cup Final day. Sheldon Rovers
were playing West Cross United.
Dave Brown, Sheldon's manager,
led his team out. It was his last day
in charge.

Dave sat next to Joe Ford,
Sheldon's coach.

"This is going to be a real test," said Joe.
"West Cross United are a strong team."

The game kicked off.

Both teams were nervous.

There were lots of mistakes.

Robbie made some poor passes.

Danny lost the ball.

Tom, who was Sheldon's keeper,

dropped an easy cross.

West Cross upped their game.

They forced a corner.

Ledley, who was Sheldon's defender,
jumped. He headed the ball. But he
nearly scored against his own team!

"Come on!" said Kyle, who was Sheldon's Captain. "We've got to do this for the boss."

He upped his game. He won headers and tackles.

Then Robbie hit a long pass to Danny.
Danny beat the fullback and crossed.

Naz leapt and headed the ball.
It looked like a certain goal…
but the keeper made a great save.
Dave Brown put his head in his hands.

At half-time it was nil-nil.

"Come on. We can win this," said Dave.

Sheldon started the second half well.
They scored with their first attack.
Robbie and Naz played a one-two
and Robbie beat the goalie.
It was 1-0 to Sheldon.

West Cross came back at Sheldon.

But Ledley defended well.

Danny worked hard on the wing.

Tom made some great saves.

Dave Brown was chewing madly.

"How long, Joe?" he asked.

"Five minutes," said Joe.

"Keep going, Sheldon!" Dave cried.

West Cross got a corner.

Their keeper went up for it.

The ball came over.

Tom punched the ball.

It hit West Cross's keeper and went in!

West Cross had scored!
Dave Brown fell to his knees.
He couldn't believe it!
At full-time it was 1-1.

Freestylers

Extra time came and went.
The score stayed one all.
The game went to penalties.

Joe Ford made a list of penalty takers.

He gave it to the ref.

Dave Brown was white with nerves.

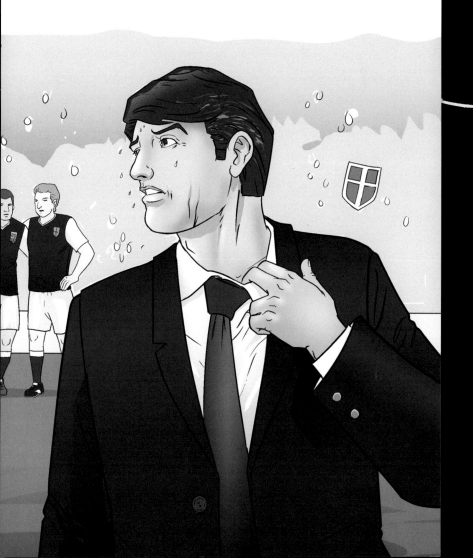

West Cross took the first penalty.

Tom saved it.

Then Robbie scored. Then West Cross scored. Next up was Naz who scored. West Cross scored again. So did Zoltan.

But Ledley missed. It was now 3–3.
The teams had one kick each to go.

West Cross went next.

Tom saved again!

It was all up to Kyle.

He put the ball on the spot.

The keeper jumped up and down.

The West Cross Fans whistled.

Dave Brown couldn't look.

Kyle took a deep breath. He ran forward.

He booted the ball hard.

It crashed high into the net.

Sheldon had won the Cup!

The players hugged each other.
Dave and Joe ran over to them.
"That was for you, boss," said Kyle.

Minutes later the players got their medals.

Kyle lifted the Cup.

The Sheldon fans cheered.

Then they carried Dave on
a lap of honour.
It was the perfect ending.

Read more stories about Sheldon Rovers.

Sheldon Rovers have made it to the Cup final. It is their manager Dave Brown's last match. Will Danny, Robby, Naz, Ledley and Tom play their best? Can they make Dave's day and win the Cup?

Danny is playing his first match for Sheldon Rovers. It is the first round of the Cup. He needs to play well to keep his place. But will nerves get the better of him?

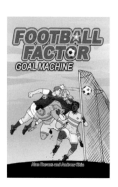

Naz is Sheldon Rover's top scorer. He is a goal machine. But suddenly things start to go wrong. He can't score at all. He loses his place in the team. Will he ever get his goal touch back?

Tom plays in goal for Sheldon Rovers. He has a lucky horseshoe that he takes to every match. But on Cup semi-final day it goes missing. Things start to go wrong. Has Tom's luck run out?

Robby keeps getting sent off. Now he has got a three-match ban and he feels down. Can he learn to control his temper? Will he ever get back in the team?

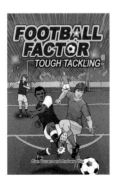

Ledley is a defender for Sheldon Rovers. He has been out injured for months. His first game is the Cup quarter final. Will he last the game? Will his tackling be strong enough?

FOR TEACHERS

About Freestylers

Freestylers is a series of carefully levelled stories, especially geared for struggling readers of both sexes. With very low reading age and high interest age, these books are humorous, fun, up-to-the-minute and edgy. Core characters provide familiarity in all of the stories, build confidence and ease pupils from one story through to the next, accelerating reading progress.

Freestylers can be used for both guided and independent reading. To make the most of the books you can:

- Focus on making each reading session successful. Talk about the text before the pupil starts reading. Introduce the characters, the storyline and any unfamiliar vocabulary.

- Encourage the pupil to talk about the book during reading and after reading. How would they have felt if they were one of the characters playing for Sheldon Rovers? How would they have dealt with the situations that the players found themselves in?

- Talk about which parts of the story they like best and why.

For guidance, this story has been approximately measured to:

National Curriculum Level: 1B   ATOS: 1.7
Reading Age: 6   Lexile ® Measure [confirmed]: 290L
Book Band: Orange